Destined To Be Loved

Sasha Mae

Sasha Mae Publishing

Sasha Mae Publishing

ISBN: 978-0-578-18459-3

PRINTED IN THE UNITED STATES OF AMERICA

CONTENTS

INTRO

Looking back at my life makes me see how truly blessed I am! You think you know the trials and tribulations one goes through. But in all reality you have no idea. A book cover speaks volumes but it doesn't tell a story. To know someone's pain, you must first walk in their shoes. Life wasn't easy for me growing up; so much hurt and pain. But you know the saying, "Nothing lasts forever." With God all hurt and pain surely comes to an end. I learned how to stand! In the process I found myself. I am who I am. You either hate it or love it!

Love,
Destiny Jones

This Is My Story...

1

THE BEGINNING

It all started on February 15, 1973 in Richmond, Virginia. I was born in Halifax County to two teen parents: Rosemary Smith, who was 15, and Desmond Jones, who was 16 at the time. They named me Destiny Jones—DJ for short because my father always wanted a boy. Even though my parents were young, they did the best that they could do to raise me. My mother was a waitress at a small restaurant called "Mama's" on Jones Drive. I called it "Ghetto Drive," where you see nothing but black folks out just kicking it. Trying to better themselves and being happy with what they had. You see, it really wasn't ghetto at all—it was like home. She was making minimum wage, and back then minimum wage for waitresses was only $2.15; now you try to make a living with that. She got up every morning and went to work. She used to wake me up before she left just to tell me that she loved me. I mean I was only a little girl but that meant a lot. She used to say, "Sweet Peaches, Momma's going to work and I want you to continue being Sweet Peaches for Momma." I never knew why she called me "Sweet Peaches" but I didn't care—we were one big happy family.

My father was a hustler; he did what he had to do so

we could survive. He used to stand on the corner selling bud (weed/marijuana)—basically whatever he could get his hands on. He was in and out of jail my whole life, all because of his lifestyle. Even though my father was in and out of jail I still felt close to him; I loved him. While my parents were out doing what they had to do I was at school—and I say it like that because I hated it! It wasn't because I wasn't smart; I was an "A" student. I went to Mercy Elementary just three blocks away from my house. I walked to school every morning by myself—well, with Grandma Betty. Grandma Betty was my mother's grandma too. She watched me while my mother and father were out and about doing them. She was a quiet old lady who really didn't say much of anything. The only time she really spoke to me was when I was at the fence going into school. She would yell, "Good luck," and I would yell back, "Bye, Nanny," and soon after, all the drama with school would begin.

Kids picked on me all the time. I was bigger than most kids that were five and six, and even taller than most. I even got picked on for my skin complexion, and I thought, ***the blacker the berry, the sweeter the juice***—well I guess not! I got teased so bad; they called me "Fatty Patty," "Big Bird," "Double Chin," "Midnight"—everything in the book. I used to cry all the time because I just didn't understand how people could do something like that to another human being; and that's when I realized it was for no reason at all. I was just different! I always felt safe at home. When I got home it would just be me and Grandma Betty watching soap opera. Well, soap opera watching Grandma Betty. Grandma Betty always slept through it. I hated TV because that would be the only thing on. But when I did I would sneak and watch Snoopy; you know, the Charlie Brown show. I used to love that show, but I never got to finish it. Grandma Betty wasn't a heavy sleeper; she used to get up on the drop of a dime and make me turn it back. Those were the good old days; she always made me laugh. I remember one day coming home from school and not seeing Grandma Betty there. It was October 31, 1981; I was excited that day and couldn't wait to get home from school. It was Halloween and Grandma Betty was taking me trick-or-treating. I was going as a princess, which I hated; I wanted to be Little Red Riding Hood. But my mother thought it was cute and that's all that mattered.

I had no idea that was going to be the day my whole life would be turned upside down. When I came home from school my mother and father both were home, which was crazy; they were never home, and definitely not at the same time. So I knew it was something serious. My Grandma Betty had died. I was too young to understand, but I knew that my life would be changed forever just by the way my mother had taken it. You see, my mother never knew her parents. Grandma Betty raised her; and my father—well that's a whole other story. After my Grandma Betty's death, my mother just went into total shock. She let herself go and even went on temporary leave from her job. My father started staying out all types of nights and I really didn't understand why. Life seemed to be really going downhill. Both of my parents were going into a depression. My mother turned into a zombie and my father turned into a drug addict—well, a crackhead in my eyes. It lasted for months, but I didn't see what happened next coming. On my ninth birthday I got the shock of my life when my mother told me that she was leaving my father. I didn't know what to say; well I was too young to really say much. But I wanted it to go back to the way it was. Before my father left, he gave me my own personal diary. I didn't know what to do with it at first, but as time went on I figured it out.

When my father left, my mother seemed to be cool with it; she started going back out with her friends and leaving me home all alone. I stayed home by myself eating bread and drinking water. I couldn't turn on the stove or even knew how to work one. About a month went by and I realized I hadn't seen my mother in a while. She was always going out; and my father just left and didn't even think to turn back around. I thought life couldn't get "Any Worse," and that's when I knew I'd spoken too soon. It was Valentine's Day, the day before my tenth birthday—which I hated! I never felt special on my birthdays; It was just another ordinary day. I remember coming home from school and seeing a car in the driveway, which was crazy because neither my mother nor her friends had cars. So I went in the house to see who it was, and it was a woman I'd never seen before. She was a pretty woman; she was taller than most women, I can tell you that, and had a shape like a model. She was dressed in a suit, and I'm talking about a man's suit. She didn't look or act like a woman; she reminded me of my father.

My mother was in her room getting dressed. When she came out, she looked so beautiful and had this glow about her. I was happy to see her with a smile on her face. She was wearing a red dress with her grandmother's pearls, which she only wore on special occasions. I didn't know where they were going but it had to be somewhere nice. When she came out she introduced us; the woman spoke first. She said, "Hi, DJ." I was looking like "how do you know my name?" and she told me her name was Moe. I just stood there looking at her; I didn't know what to think. My mother told me they were going out to dinner. I wanted to go! My mother and I hadn't had dinner together in months. She was always either working or just out doing her thing. Moe even wanted me to go; but my mother said no, it's grownup night… "if you know what I mean"—talking to Moe.

As they were leaving, my mother pulled me to the side to tell me she had something to talk to me about when she came home! I didn't know what she was going to say; I was hoping she would have told me my father was coming home. I woke up at 3 am from noises I heard coming out of my mother's room. I heard someone talking and laughing; I thought it was my father. I was scared of the dark so I didn't get up at first. I called my mother three times and she didn't answer me. I didn't know what had happened—one minute it sounded like someone was there and then the next minute it sounded like no one else was in the house. I was starting to get more and more scared by the second, so I decided to get up and see what was going on. As I was walking out of my room I really couldn't see, but I at least knew where my mother's room was. Her room was on the same side as mine; the bathroom was in between both rooms. When I approached my mother's room her door was closed; so I put my ear to the door to see if I could hear anything, but I heard nothing. I opened the door just in time to see my mother and Moe both lying there naked!

2

OUT OF THE CLOSET

(Entering Diary) ...

Dear Diary,
Ever feel like your whole world's just been flipped upside down? I'm dealing with the shock of my life, and honestly I'm not fully understanding what's going on! My mom with a girl; isn't that wrong? In my princess books I always see Prince Charming, not Princess Charming! How do I deal with another wrong that just can't be right? I can't tell anyone, especially at school. I'm already getting teased; I'll be the laughingstock of the whole school. Why me? Why now? Life just can't get any worse!

(Exiting Diary) ...

I sat there looking up at the ceiling as my mother was trying to explain things to me; but I really didn't want to hear it. Ever watch the Charlie Brown show and you always notice when the teacher talks it's like "womb, womb, womb"; you just don't get it! That's when I realized how different I truly was. She kept asking me if I understood what she was saying while she was telling me at the same time Moe was moving in. All I could do was say to myself, why did it have to happen to me? I just nodded yes to everything and she stated "Good" and left, while I sat there confused.

A few weeks went by and I started to really like Moe. She was mad cool and she liked the same things I did, plus she was always home with me. My mom worked 12 hours or more a day; sometimes she wouldn't get home until after I was already in bed sleeping, but when I was up that's when all the drama would start. I guess my mother was expecting to come home to a hot-cooked meal every night, and when she didn't boy was she angry. My stepmother—or should I just call her Moe? —would start blaming things on me. She used to say, "If it wasn't for DJ having me tend to her every need all day long, maybe I would have a hot cooked meal ready for you." She would also say, "Do you think it's easy being with her all day? She talks too much and stays in my way." Not once did my mother ever stick up for me, nor did she tell her to watch her mouth about her "Sweet Peaches." I just didn't understand what went wrong with me and my mother's relationship.

They argued all the time; I didn't see why my mother was even with her. At the end of the summer of '85, a week before my graduation from Mercy Elementary, I got another big surprise. I went to school that morning like every other morning and did what I had to do and left. But this day was different! I came home from school and walked in to the house to see this man sitting on my couch. He started smiling at me as I continued walking through the door. He started talking about how big I done got and how he'd missed me. I couldn't pinpoint who he was at first because he looked older in the face and his skin seemed so wrinkled like he'd been through some rough times in his days. But when I started to walk closer and closer to where he was sitting, I just knew it was my daddy. I wasn't happy at all to see him; I was pissed. After all these years he was finally back in my life, and what could I say to the man who'd just up and left me?

(Entering Diary) ...

Dear Diary,
My father's back! Every time I think that I done figured something out I find out that I don't know anything at all. My mother was straight upfront with me; she told me at the end of the week I was going to stay with him. Who's "him"? I don't know this man, he hasn't been in my life for the past 7 years, and she wants me to just pack up my things like nothing ever happened. I feel like my mother's just trying to push me out of the way so she can just be with Moe! I don't think he's really a changed man. What did I do to deserve this? God, if you hear me please don't do this to me.

(Exiting Diary) ...

The next day my mother tells me about a dinner with my father—or should I say my sperm donor? I go; well, I didn't have any choice. He didn't take me anywhere special, just to McDonald's, which happened to be just around the corner. He was so cheap, he ordered me a Happy Meal. I was looking like, "What am I, eight?!" We talked and I started to forgive him bit by bit. I mean I at least felt a little more comfortable with the fact I was going with him for the summer. He lived in Brooklyn, New York. I was excited, as I'd never been to the city. Well anywhere outside of Virginia. The week before it was time for me to go with my father went by fast. I was so excited that I had my bags packed three days before. It was my first big vacation so I was ready. I took a plane for the first time by myself because my father left the same night we went to McDonald's. I mean I didn't care—it was kind of cool.

The whole time on the plane I started to have mixed feelings about everything once again. I didn't really know him or trust him. He was a complete stranger. I was just hoping that he was a changed man like he said he was. If not it kind of wouldn't be anything new, because he'd already betrayed me in a way that he could never take back. Don't get me wrong I love my daddy but I'm hurt by his actions. I can't wait until the summer is over!

3

THE SUMMER OF '85

When I arrived in Brooklyn it was even more exciting. It was bigger than I'd thought. The plane ride was a little crazy; my ears kept popping the whole time. My father didn't pick me up from the airport; he actually made me take a cab. I didn't care, though; I enjoyed the cab ride. The whole time I was looking out the window seeing so much going on. New York City is so big and busy. I'd never thought or even dreamed of ever being somewhere like this; it's really, truly a city that never sleeps. I pulled up to this building—well this storefront that had these guys in front selling. I knew exactly what they were doing immediately. It was the same type of lifestyle my father was in all those years. As I was getting out of the cab, one of the guys that was standing out there came up and approached me. He asked me was my name DJ; I didn't know him but I still told him yeah. He paid my cab fare and told me that he was my father's friend Ant. He told me that my father went somewhere for a minute and would be back soon. I didn't say anything; I just nodded okay as we began walking up three flights of stairs.

My father's friend Ant was nice; I'd never seen him

before, but I figured my father must have met him in the city. He was a tall Puerto Rican man with braids that were so long they went halfway down his back; plus, he was a cutie. He showed me around my father's little two-bedroom apartment even though everything was right there. It was the smallest apartment I had ever seen, and I knew it was something new for my father too. Soon after showing me around, he went back outside to do what he did. He informed me before he left that he and my father would be back. I was clueless about my father having a roommate, and if my mother had known she definitely would not have let this go down. Hours went by and neither my father nor his friend had gotten home yet. When they did show up it was 4 o'clock in the morning. They seemed drunk, high, or maybe even both. Ant went straight to his room while my father sat on the couch with me, telling me how happy he was I was there and how he was sorry for not picking me up from the airport. After he sat there apologizing for five minutes, he went to bed and so did I.

When I woke up Ant was in the living room watching TV. I didn't know where my father was, but in my heart I knew he wasn't going to be there when I woke up. Ant was showing me more love than my own father. Ant told me that he was taking me sightseeing in the Big Apple. I was so excited! He took me all over. I saw so much: "Madison Square Garden," "Times Square," "World Trade Center," "Restaurants"—everything that you could have dream of. By the time we got back, I was so tired out that I just went straight to sleep. The next day I woke up to someone cooking in the kitchen; I got up to see who it was, and it was my father. I just stood there; I couldn't believe he was home, and especially making breakfast. As soon as he saw me standing there, he told me that he had something to tell me and he wanted me to sit down at the table so we could talk. He informed me that he was not going to be home for the next couple days because he was going to New Jersey to visit some friends. I asked if I could go but he told me it was an important business trip that wasn't going to take long, so I couldn't go.

The whole time he was talking I just couldn't help myself but to think about my mother, and how she hadn't called me at all. Not even to just make sure I got to New York safe. I guess she really did just want to get rid of me. I felt so hurt and betrayed. The two people that are supposed to love you turned their backs on me. As my father was getting ready to go, Ant came out of his room with nothing but boxers on, which was very surprising. But right then and there I knew something was up.

4

ANOTHER WRONG THAT JUST CAN'T BE RIGHT

My father kissed me on my forehead and said his good-byes. In a way I was kind of happy he was leaving. Once again it was just me and Ant. Ant just sat there looking at me like I was a piece of meat that went bad. I sat there watching TV until I fell asleep. I had to have been sleeping for a while, because when I woke up it was dark out. Ant wasn't there when I woke up; he was still outside "getting his hustle on," so he said. I got up to make me something to eat and to take a shower. After that, I just continued watching TV; I mean there wasn't anything else to do. I had no friends and didn't know anybody, so my hobby was eating and watching TV; some hobby that was. I fell back to sleep shortly after, and woke up the next morning around 8:23. I felt something or someone on top of me.

When I opened up my eyes, Ant was on top of me as if something was about to go down. I asked him what he was doing and to get off of me. He just continued lying on top of me with a blank stare as if I had done something wrong. I asked him repeatedly to get off of me. He must have been high because he'd never done anything like this before. I tried to push him off of me but he was too strong.

He started to then try and pull down my shorts. I began crying and pleading with him to stop, but he just continued pulling on my clothes. He wasn't saying anything; it was like he was a totally different person. I kept screaming and crying, "Stop, don't, you're hurting me"; the next thing I knew he had pinned me down on the couch with my panties and shorts ripped off. I was still trying to fight and get him off of me, but I couldn't; I was only 12. He started to stick his thing in me. All I could remember is this sharp pain down there; it felt like my whole body was being ripped right open. I continued screaming and crying as I was fighting him with all I had. I'd never felt so used and abused in my whole life.

It lasted for hours; I couldn't believe he had done something like this to me. I'd trusted him. After he was done he got up and told me to go in the bathroom and clean myself up. I ran in the bathroom and locked the door; I was so scared and drained. I had blood everywhere; I'd never seen so much blood in my life. I hurt so bad I could barely move; the pain was so unbearable. I lay on the bathroom floor for hours, crying and praying that my mother would come and get me. As time went by I got the courage to get up. I went out in the living room just to get my diary, which was in my book bag. I was scared, but I knew no one was there. Ant had left an hour before. I grabbed my diary and ran back into the bathroom and locked the door. I then began writing in my diary, which I hadn't written in since I'd got there.

(Entering Diary) ...

Dear Diary,
I can't believe what just happened; I never knew that something like this would ever happen to me. I mean I trusted Ant; I'm only 12. Even though I'm bigger and taller

than most kids my age doesn't mean this had to happen. I'm ready to go home; why doesn't anybody love me? My father doesn't want to spend time with me and my own mother doesn't even call to see if I'm okay and the guy I thought was there for me hurt me in a way I can't explain. God please help me—I want to go home!

(Exiting Diary) ...

I slept in the bathroom that night; I didn't want Ant to come back and hurt me again. It was 5:20 in the morning when there was a knock on the bathroom door; it was Ant. He kept yelling and screaming, "Open the door." I was scared and felt all alone; my father was nowhere to be found and my mother was all the way in Virginia, and she couldn't even pick up the phone to check up on me. I didn't say anything as he continued yelling and knocking on the door for about an hour; then he finally gave up.

The next morning around 10 o'clock I decided to get out of the bathroom; I thought Ant was gone, but I was wrong. It was like he was sitting by the door waiting for me to come out. When I did he grabbed me and threw me on the couch and had his way with me. It seemed like no matter how much I screamed and cried it didn't work—the situation just got more and more intense. After he was done, he had the nerve to tell me not to tell anyone. He let me know if I did it wouldn't matter because no one would believe me anyway. As he was telling me all of that bull, I believed it. It was obvious no one cared about me. All I could do was cry. I kept asking him why he would hurt me without having any remorse. But he just sat there looking at me with this blank stare; he couldn't explain himself. I just got up and ran back into the bathroom before he could even think about having round two.

I sat in the bathroom and cried myself to sleep. The next morning there was another knock on the door, but this time it was my father. I couldn't believe it. I blamed him because he put his own daughter in this situation and wasn't there for me once again in my life. I opened the door with tears in my eyes; all I could say to him was that I wanted to go home. He just stood there confused; he had no idea what had happened just hours before. He told me to get dressed because he wanted to take me out to eat. I did, but in a way I still didn't care whether he was there or not—he was useless.

We went to McDonald's once again, but this time he let me get whatever I wanted. As we sat in McDonald's eating, I just sat there in silence. I had nothing else to say to him. He kept telling me how sorry he was for leaving me, and that the remainder of my vacation would be our time. I just sat there praying that God would make a way for me to go back home with my mother. After we were done eating, we went back to his apartment and watched movies together. That was the most time I'd got out of my father since being there. Ant was nowhere to be found when my father came back; I just didn't bother telling my father what had happened because I believed Ant when he told me nobody would believe me. Two days later there was a heavy knock on the door. I was just sitting in the living room watching TV while my father was in the kitchen making us lunch. It was my mother; I was so shocked to see her. She came to the city to get me. She'd found out that my father hadn't stopped doing drugs like he said he had. I was so happy to see her. My father just sat there looking puzzled and lost. My mother said what she had to say to him and we left.

I cried all the way back home. My mother didn't know why, but she kept saying "stop crying" and that she was happy to see me too; so I took it as she just thought it was because I missed her. I mean I did but that wasn't just it. When we got back home I never told anyone about the situation—not even my own mother.

5

SOMETHING NEW

(Entering Diary) ...

I'm so glad to be home. This summer was the worst summer ever. Some father I have, but most of all some friend that he has. Why did this have to happen to me? I'm just happy I got out of the situation. I'm starting middle school soon and I'm excited and nervous at the same time. I'm just going to have to bury the summer of '85 forever.

(Exiting Diary) ...

Three weeks later I started Virginia Bee's Middle School. Since day one I was nervous; I didn't know what to expect. All I knew was that it was so many people; it was nothing like elementary school. The first day was a little crazy. I couldn't find any of my classes. Every time I walked down the halls it was like all eyes were on me. I can remember people staring and giving me dirty looks. I figured it was because of my weight. I was a size 20–22 in the 7th grade; the only thing that was appealing about me was my hair. I had beautiful long jet-black hair that everyone gave me compliments on. I never thought I was going to make friends. A few weeks into school someone new came into my life. It was my last-period class, which was my math class. Some girl that I'd never seen before came strolling in and sat by me! She actually spoke to me, which was so surprising; no one ever wanted to say anything to me, and when they did it wasn't anything nice.

Her name was Jasmine Bombers—Jazzy for short. She was totally opposite from me; she was skinny, real tall, and even taller than me, with beautiful caramel skin. We became friends that same day and did everything together. I finally knew what it felt like to have a friend. Well she ended up being more to me—she was my best friend, my walking diary, but most of all my sister I'd never had. She was the only child and so was I. We spent a lot of our time together. She stayed at my house from time to time and I stayed at hers. Even though we were best friends and told each other our deepest secrets, I never thought about telling her what happened to me the summer of '85. But down the line she found out anyways.

It was a day I brought my diary to school with me; that day I received my first "F" in one of my classes. So I took my diary out of my book bag to express how I felt about getting an "F." After class I left my diary on my desk by mistake, and that day Jazzy was the last one out of class. So she picked it up and brought it home with her. When she was home she happened to open it and read the part about the summer I went to my father's house. I didn't even realize at first that I'd left it until she called me that night. She was upfront about it, asking me if I was all right and did I tell anyone about what happened. I was shocked; I thought no one would ever find out. But at the same time I was happy it was finally out and she was the one that knew about it.

After that night we never spoke about it again; she knew how upset I got when we did, and she didn't want me to hurt over it anymore. I started opening up to her more and more, and so did she. I even told her how I'd never had a boyfriend and how I wanted one just to know how it felt. But who knew in the 8th grade my dreams would come true. It was October 5, 1986, a year since Jazzy and I conversation. I went over to Jazzy's house after school because her family was having a little get-together for her aunt and cousin that were moving to Virginia from Atlanta, Georgia. When I got there I couldn't find Jazzy; but I did spot some boy posted up on the wall as I was walking in. When I finally did find Jazzy, he was the first person she introduced me to.

His name was Matt. He was her first cousin—her aunt's son. I was so shy and nervous; I didn't know how to act around him. All I knew was that someone like him wasn't going to be interested in a girl like me; but I was wrong. We started dating a little while after. I couldn't believe I finally had a boyfriend, let alone an older one. You see I was in the 8th grade and he was in the 10th; but I wasn't worried because my best friend was his cousin and we told each other everything. We dated while I was in middle school and high school. I felt like I was in love and had finally found the right one for me. Even when he went off to college, we still were close.

High school was just as good as middle school, and Jazzy and I were still closer than ever. But high school went by even faster than middle school. Before we knew it we were seniors.

6

IN AND OUT

April 13, 1991—the day of our senior prom. Jazzy and I were at my house getting dressed and ready for our big day. We were so excited! I had on a green dress that went a little below my knees, with flat pumps. I didn't like how I looked, but it really didn't matter—prom only comes once in a lifetime. Jazzy, on the other hand, looked beautiful as usual. She was wearing a short red dress with some red high-heel shoes. When we were done getting dressed, our mothers and Moe took pictures of us. I hated taking pictures; I felt like I was too big for all of that. I was happy when Matt finally blew the horn five minutes later, letting us know he was outside. Jazzy went to the prom with one of Matt's roommates from school. His name was Will, and he wasn't as good looking as Matt, but whenever Will and Jazzy were together they always looked like the perfect couple. We didn't have enough money to get a limo, so Matt's mother let us take her new 1991 Honda Accord to the prom. If you ask me, I was happy we didn't get a limo; I didn't want to put so much attention on how I was looking in the first place. Even though everyone else thought I looked nice.

As soon as we arrived at the prom, we went straight to the dance floor. We stayed on the dance floor the whole entire night. When it was time to finally leave the prom, we went to Motel 6. For years' seniors had a tradition where after prom whoever and their dates would go to Motel 6 and make it do what it do—if you know what I mean. Jazzy and Will had their own room, and Matt and I had ours. I was so nervous! I knew the night of my senior prom would be the night I lost my virginity. Matt and I were in love. Before Matt and I had sex, I let him know about the summer of '85. My deepest secret. He told me he loved me and wouldn't do anything to hurt me if only I gave him a chance; and I did. Deep down inside I trusted him. That night we had sex or made love (whatever you want to call it), but I still didn't feel complete. Maybe it was because he really wasn't the one that God sent for me. After we were done doing what we did, he fell asleep, while I sat up writing in my diary that I'd brought along for the ride.

(Entering Diary) ...

Tonight was the night that I finally lost my virginity to the man of my dreams. Ever want something so bad that you do anything to get it? But when you get that thing that you wanted so bad, you still don't feel complete. I don't know why I feel the way that I do, because this is definitely something that I wanted. But I still feel empty inside! Well enough about this; overall I had a great time and I hope Will and Jazzy did as well. I can't wait until tomorrow so my girl and I can have our special talk like we always do. I just love my best friend; I wouldn't trade her for the world. This will definitely be a night to remember!

(Exiting Diary) ...

The next morning, we all got up and went out to breakfast. We went to Friendly's—one of Matt's favorite spots. While we were there, we talked about our prom experience and how the four of us needed to spend more time together. As we were finishing up our food, I noticed Jazzy didn't look so good. I asked her if she was okay and she just responded back that it was nothing and she just needed more sleep. I didn't believe her because I knew her in and out. It looked like it was more than what she was telling me, but I just said "okay" and left it at that. As we were getting ready to get in the car, Jazzy just collapsed and went unconscious. We called 911 immediately. While we waited for them to come we tried waking Jazzy up, but it was no use. I began to cry my eyes out! Out of all these years I'd never even seen Jazzy with a cold; I was terrified. I drove in the ambulance with Jazzy while Matt and Will went to go get Jazzy's mother.

The whole time in the ambulance I held on to her hand. I just couldn't look at her. When we got to the hospital, they made me wait in the waiting room until her family came. Her family all walked in the hospital a half an hour later in tears. We sat there for hours while the doctor ran tests on her to see exactly what was going on. When the doctor finally did come to the waiting room to tell us what was going on, it wasn't what we were expecting. He informed us that Jazzy's cancer had come back and it didn't look good. When I heard "cancer" I lost it; I couldn't lose her—she was all I had. Jazzy had to stay in the hospital so they could continue to see what they could do for her. I didn't know what to do. After hearing the bad news, I asked Matt to take me home; I couldn't take it anymore. That night I couldn't sleep—Jazzy was too much on my mind. I just sat up crying and writing in my diary.

(Entering Diary) ...

I can't believe this is happening! My best friend has cancer!?! How is this even possible? Why wouldn't she tell me? We told each other everything! We just were at our senior prom having a blast—now this. I can't lose her! She's all I have. Why when I think everything seems to be going good something has to come crashing down on me! This is too much for me right now. Why?? Why me? Why Her? Haven't we been through enough! God, please don't do this to me. Protect her like only you can!

(Exiting Diary) ...

The next day Matt came and got me so I could visit Jazzy. When we got there, the doctor was informing Jazzy's mother about other things they'd observed. He informed her that Jazzy's liver and kidneys were affected, and they were shutting down. He also told us that she only had a couple weeks to live. Everyone broke down in tears; her mother took it the hardest. I can remember hearing Jazzy's mother screaming, **"No, not my baby,"** as tears flowed from her eyes. I was in total shock once again; I couldn't take the pain. We were graduating in a few weeks and were supposed to be going away to college. I felt like a piece of me was dying; I just needed to see my best friend. The doctor allowed us to see her, but it had to be one at a time. Jazzy's mother went in first. When it was my time to see her, I had tears running down my face. When I walked into her room she was sitting up watching TV. She informed me that she didn't want me to be upset because where she was going would be a better place than this evil world we lived in now. I broke down even more; I didn't want her to go anywhere. I wanted her to stay with me forever! I walked over to her and gave her a big hug and kiss on her forehead.

I sat in the chair on the side of her bed and talked to her for hours, reminiscing about our good and bad times and how we overcame our hardships in life through it all. We both ended up falling asleep. An hour or two later, Matt came in the room and woke me up so he could take me home. I kissed Jazzy and told her good night. I didn't have any energy when I got home to write in my diary so I just went straight to bed!

7

WHY, GOD?

I woke up the next morning at 5:13 from noises coming from my mother's room. I got up to see what was going on. When I walked in her room she was on the floor crying; I knew it was something serious. All I could think about was Jazzy. I walked in and immediately asked Moe what was going on; but she didn't respond right away. It was like she was mute, or maybe it was the fact that she had no idea how to break the bad news to me. She turned around towards where I was and began telling me how sorry she was. In all those years I'd never seen Moe shed one tear. I didn't want to hear what was coming next. Moe told me that Jazzy had died an hour before, and that Matt was going to take me to the hospital to see her one last time if I wanted to go. I was speechless; I couldn't believe she was gone. I ran in my room and slammed the door shut. I had to write about this in my diary.

(Entering Diary) ...

I can't believe it! I lost the only one that was ever there for me. This is not fair; what am I going to do!?!? I don't think I can face this! How could you let this happen, God!!!! I guess you lied, Jazzy; you told me you would always be there for me! You're a liar! I need you right now and you're nowhere to be found. How could you leave me?!?! Why wouldn't you tell me, I thought we told each other everything? I'm so angry! Why??? Why??? Please, God, don't do this! I want her back!

(Exiting Diary) ...

I ended up calling Matt and telling him not to come and pick me up. I needed time; I slept the whole entire day away. The next day I got up and went to Jasmine's house. They were having a little something over there for her. When I got there I couldn't do it. Seeing all her family hurting, and seeing pictures of her all over made me sick. I ended up going home shortly after; I was hurting so bad. You can never predict the future—only God knows. I kept my distance from everyone until the funeral. The day of the funeral, I rode with my mother and Moe. When we got there, there were so many people. I didn't realize how many people Jazzy actually knew in her lifetime. As soon as I walked in the church, I wanted to walk right back out. I broke down in tears. I couldn't look at her in a casket. I sat in the back of the church the entire service; my body felt numb. When the service was over I went straight home; I couldn't watch someone throw dirt on my best friend. I was completely broken inside. She was gone and there was nothing I could do about it.

Two weeks later was our graduation, but I wasn't excited. That day was supposed to be for me and Jazzy, and it didn't feel right without her being there. I missed her so much! I hadn't seen Matt since the funeral, but I didn't care. I couldn't deal with anyone, especially the man that was her first cousin. A week after graduation I called Matt; I was starting to miss him. But every time I would call he wouldn't answer. A few days later he finally decided to call me back. I was so happy. But the conversation that we had was not pretty. He told me that he didn't want to be with me anymore, and that he'd found a real woman on his college campus. I just said okay and hung up. I didn't know what to say. I couldn't believe the words that were even coming out of his mouth. He knew how close Jazzy and I were, so I couldn't understand why he wasn't understanding about the fact I took it hard. I felt betrayed once again by a man I'd thought I could trust. After I got off the phone with him, I began to cry my eyes out while I wrote in my diary.

(Entering Diary) ...

How could Matt do this to me??? Talking about he wants a real woman, not a little girl. He couldn't even wait to tell me he was seeing someone else, and leaving me. He knew that I took Jazzy's death hard, and I just needed time. I loved him and never would have thought he would have played me at a time that I needed him the most. I don't know what I'm going to do! Everyone that I ever loved is now gone. Even though the hardest thing to do is to move on, I have to do what I have to do. I'm just going to have to accept it! God, you truly work in mysterious ways. I don't know how you do things or even why you allow things to happen, but I guess I'm just going to have to deal with it. Questioning you and not getting an answer is not helping me! Maybe everything that's been happening is for the best, even though I can't see it. This college experience should be fun. A new start is definitely needed! Good luck to me!

(Exiting Diary) ...

8

BACK AT THE BEGINNING

When I arrived in Brooklyn, New York, I was so excited but nervous at the same time. I didn't know what to expect. Brooklyn University was okay, but brochures always made something seem bigger or better than what it was. I wish Jazzy were here to see it; I know she would have loved it. I miss her so much! I know this experience is either going to make me or break me. I finally was getting my new start and I was ready for it. I brought a picture of Jazzy with me. I knew she would be my good-luck charm to keep me moving forward in this cold world. The first couple of days were crazy. All my classes were all over the place. I thought high school was bad. As time went on my roommate was starting to be more and more cool—well for a white girl at least. You see I never really hung out with anyone outside of my race before. I wasn't racist or anything, they just never crossed my path and vice versa. The South was definitely different from the North. For the first time in my life since losing Jazzy, I felt okay. It was sad that I was in New York City, and couldn't reach out to my father. My father only lived seven or eight blocks away from the school. In a way I didn't really care; I was completely done with him. To this day I still don't know whether or not he knew I attended a college in Brooklyn. But I was there whether he knew it or not, and I wasn't planning on leaving. Before I knew it, I had been in Brooklyn a whole two months. I was making new friends and doing great in all of my classes. There was nothing that was going to stop me—until I bumped into this guy from high school named Josh, who I actually had a mean crush on back in the day. You see I never told anyone I had a crush on him, not even Jazzy. I guess we both didn't tell each other everything. It was crazy because in those four years we never even spoke. But for some strange reason we talked to each other like we always had a conversation. We talked about everything; well at least we tried. It really wasn't much to talk about, so we decided after class we would get up and talk over dinner. I was shocked but excited at the same time. I couldn't wait until class was over. When I walked out of class, he was right there at the door waiting for me. It was so unexpected! I didn't even have time to go to my dorm room to freshen up. We didn't end up going anywhere special, though. For some strange reason all the guys that I knew in my life always took me to McDonald's. I guess that was all I was worth; well that's how I felt.

We sat there and talked for about an hour about school, and how he also had a crush on me. After we were done eating, we walked through Central Park. I'd never felt so nervous in my life from just walking with a guy. It was something different and special about him, or maybe it was some type of cover-up to get over Matt. After our walk through the park, he walked me back to my dorm room and ended the night with a kiss. I probably should have slapped him, but his lips against mine felt so right. Later on that night, he called me and asked me to be his girlfriend. I didn't know what to say; everything was happening so fast. I mean I liked him, but at the same time I knew nothing about him. All I knew was that he was a fine, tall (about 6'4"), built man with beautiful dark chocolate skin.

It was a long pause on the phone, but I ended up saying yes. We stayed on the phone the whole entire night. The next day I couldn't wait to see him; he was taking me to dinner. I ended up not being able to focus in any of my classes; I couldn't stop thinking about him. He was getting the best of me already. I was happy when 4 o'clock finally came. I rushed home to get dressed and ready for our date. I never knew what to wear so I just put on one of my favorite dresses. Which happened to be my black silk dress. I loved that dress—it always made me look thinner. When it was finally time for him to show up at 6 o'clock for our date, he never did. I waited and waited; around 2:30 in the morning, he finally decided to call. I was so upset; how could he try to play me! He apologized about standing me up. But at the same time I wasn't trying to hear it. He told me he didn't show up because he was studying for this big test that he forgot about, and the test was actually in a few hours. I ended up forgiving him; I wanted it to work. A few minutes later he ended up surprising me at my dorm room. We sat up all night talking about us, and the future that we could have together.

That night he ended up staying the night with me while my roommate was out on a Friday night doing her thing. Even though Josh stayed the night in my dorm room, we didn't have sex. Once again I found myself telling another guy about what had occurred to me the summer I went to my father's house. I guess I felt as though in order for someone to have a healthy and honest relationship, it was best to tell them everything up front. He was very understanding.

By three weeks of us dating, I felt like everything was working out in my favor. It seemed like a fairy tale. He treated me so good, just like a woman should. I began to feel more and more comfortable around him, to the point I was starting to think it was maybe time to take our relationship to the next level. Every time he would touch or look at me, I would immediately get butterflies.

(Entering Diary) ...

Omg! It's just something about him that makes my body melt. I feel so in love for the first time in a very long time. He makes me completely happy! I think I have finally met the right one for me. I don't want to rush into anything, but I want him to know that I want us to work out just as much as he does. I keep asking myself, is it too soon to take our relationship to the next level or am I just cautious because of my past? I want to so bad! But maybe I am scared of being hurt and used again. No, I don't think he's that kind of man, but I realize in life people sometimes do a complete 360. I'm not saying it will happen, but you never know in this cruel world. Not only that, but I don't want to be one of them girls that sleeps with any- and everybody. Time is precious! I don't want to waste time or an opportunity to make that move. But I need my next move to definitely be my best move. Diary, sometimes I wish you could talk back to me, and give me some type of advice. I don't know what to do!

(Exiting Diary) ...

9

MY "BOO-THANG"

Before I knew it we were dating for 3 ½ months with-out having sex, and everything was going well. But it was finally time to be intimate with each other. I felt like we'd definitely waited long enough. It was on Valentine's Day when we had sex for the first time. That day he told me he had something special lined up for me. For the first time in our relationship, I was going over to his dorm room. Every time I wanted to go over to his room, it was always some excuse why I couldn't. So I figured it was a big step in our relationship.

(Entering Diary) ...

Wow, I can't believe that this is really going to happen. Josh is my knight in shining armor. I love the fact that he swept me off my feet and made me see that I could actually love again. I never saw myself being with anyone else be-sides Matt. But at the same time I'm falling in love with Josh and want him to be the one I spend the rest of my life with. I just hope and pray that I'm not moving too fast! I guess time will only tell.

(Exiting Diary) ...

I arrived at his dorm room an hour late; I was so nervous. I went for a walk around Central Park just thinking and asking myself could this really be love. He was so happy to see me that being an hour late never even crossed his mind. He had flowers for me with rose petals all over the room, with a nice big teddy bear and chocolates in the middle of the bed. I was so surprised; I felt loved. We ended up having a candlelight dinner. Chinese food was my favorite food at the time, so he made sure he had all of my favorites on the menu. He was so sweet! That night we had sex...well, made love. It was wonderful! There was something different about him, and I knew he was going to change me for good. After we were done doing what we do, we sat up for the rest of the night talking. I ended up staying the night and leaving the next morning to get ready for school. It was always so hard to focus in my classes after I'd spent romantic nights with Josh. When school was finally over, I jumped on the phone so I could hear his voice. The first couple of times he didn't answer; but I wanted to hear his voice so bad that I kept calling. When he finally did answer I was open; it felt like my heart was about to jump out and reach him on the other side of the phone. He was my boo and I was his. We talked for the rest of the day about what occurred the night before, and how he was finally glad we did what we did. Later on that night I went back over to his dorm room, but I made sure I was well rested for what was about to take place. When I arrived at his dorm room, there was no one in sight. He was hiding and came out shortly after and surprised me. We went straight into doing what we had to do (if you know what I mean). The next morning, I woke up and went back to my dorm room to get dressed and ready for my class. For about six weeks straight, sex was all our relationship consisted of. We weren't going out on dates or even having conversations like we used to. He started texting me only when he was ready to do that one thing. I had no idea why our relationship was turning out to be just a booty call; but at the same time I didn't care. I still had him right there with me even if he was only there when we were intimate.

The night before April Fool's Day I sat down with Josh to finally tell him how I felt. I let him know that I missed the old times we shared, and that I wanted to take it slower. He was upset, and really wasn't trying to hear it. He made it seem like I owed him something, or it was my job to please his every need. I was hurt! I realized right then and there that he really didn't care how I felt or even what I thought about the situation after all. I couldn't take the yelling back and forth, so I ended up just leaving. I felt good that I'd finally let someone know how I felt. Not only that, but I was happy that we didn't have sex that night. The next morning, I tried calling him to make sure everything was still good between us, but he didn't answer. I let it go; I figured he was still mad and needed more time to cool off. Around 1:30 in the morning he finally called me back—well, texted me. Once again he was apologizing for not answering my calls. He began to tell me how he still loved me, and how he needed to see me. I thought he just wanted to talk that night so I got up and walked over to his dorm room. When I got over there I realized he didn't want to talk after all, but that he wanted to do way more. I told him "No"; I was so angry that I just yelled at him and left. When I got back to my dorm room I went straight to bed. I couldn't even think straight, but I truly thank God for creating diaries.

(Entering Diary) ...

I'm so angry. How could he take what I said lightly? I feel like he's falling out of love with me and only wants me for one thing. I know I'm not important but I thought he respected me, and wanted more from this relationship. I'm so tired of feeling this way. I felt like Josh was the one, and like life was worth living and moving forward now that I'd found Josh. Now I don't know anymore...SMH...I'm tired of it just being about sex. I want more; I mean don't I deserve more? I want to be loved; and I don't think that's too much to ask for. God, please help me!!!

(Exiting Diary) ...

The next few days were the worst! Every time we saw each other, we would fight and argue. I said some things I didn't mean and so did he. We went for a week without speaking; I missed him like crazy. He didn't call or respond back to any of my messages. I didn't know if he needed more time to cool off or if he was just completely done with the relationship; I was clueless. I felt bad about the whole situation; I just wanted it to be over so we could move forward. But on April 20 I knew that I still had bad luck with men. I was walking down the hall towards the student lounge when I bumped into Josh sitting at a table with another girl; so I walked over to see what was up. He acted like he didn't even know me. He just sat there and continued his conversation with the other female. So I sat there at the table with them just to see what would happen. I kept trying to see what was going on and what his problem was with me, but he just kept trying to dismiss me. By then I realized that the person I was sitting right in front of was his new girlfriend and he had totally moved on.

I was hurt; I just stood up and walked away. I couldn't deal with another betrayal. I went back to my dorm room and just cried my eyes out. I couldn't take my heart being broken again. The next couple of weeks I couldn't even get out of bed. I ended up not going to any of my classes, so I missed my finals. I thought he loved me and wanted more out of life with me. I felt like my life was always going to be the same. I couldn't stay at the school with Josh being there, walking around with his new girlfriend. I started to think that college wasn't for me. I couldn't go back home with my mother and Moe. How couldn't it be more to life? I loved New York; but I didn't see myself staying somewhere outside of the school. I needed a place and a job ASAP.

(Entering Diary) ...

I hate my life! I wish I'd never met Josh; he hurt me so bad. I can't even think straight. I need a place and a job in about a week, before it's too late. This semester has been the worst! I miss Jazzy; I wish she were here so bad. I feel so alone with nowhere to go. I hope something happens for me before I have nothing else to do but to go back home to Virginia. Yeah, I know I shouldn't always make myself an easy target for men to walk all over me. But when you live with a void of wanting to be loved, you become desperate in life. I need help. But I'm not quite sure where to turn.

(Exiting Diary) ...

10

DOWNHILL

At this point in time I would have tried anything, I was so desperate. I decided to walk around the New York City streets to see what kind of jobs were available. There were so many people around; it was very hard to see if places were even hiring. I did see a sign that said "Hiring All Models"; I figured it was a waste of time to stop, being that I was unattractive and extremely overweight. But the guy that was holding the sign noticed how hard I was staring, and he ended up stopping me to tell me that they didn't discriminate and the pay was out of this world. So I decided to go in and check it out. I had no idea what kind of place it was, but there were so many girls walking around in bikinis. I was nervous, and I prayed no one would want to see me in one. It was dark inside; I couldn't really see as one of the girls directed me upstairs to see the owner. I soon found out that the place I was in was a private strip club. I didn't know what to say to the owner.

When I walked in the owner's office, he immediately got up out of his seat and walked around the desk to check me out. I could have told him I had nothing good going on, but I was kind of curious to hear what he had to say. When he was done doing what he did, he told me to have a seat in one of the chairs that was right across from his. He told me I was too beautiful to stand. No one had ever said anything like that to me, so it made me feel a little good about myself; I just smiled at him. He then went into explaining that the strip joint was for people that were blessed, "if you know what I mean." I knew what he meant, but at the same time Grandma Betty always told me that everyone was different. Some are big and some are small, and to see it as being blessed when you have a little extra baggage. He informed me that he had another job lined up that would be perfect for me. I was so desperate that I didn't even hesitate to say "I'll take it," even though I had no idea what kind of job it was.

He was pleased with my response and told me that I just needed to set up a six-month contract with him. He also went into telling me that the job came with free room-and-board for the first three months. I was so happy; I not only had a job lined up but a place to stay all in one. I didn't even read the contract; I just signed each and every page and the deal was done. I saw it as this: what could be worse than being a stripper, and being my size I had no chance with that. He asked me when was the soonest I could start; I told him as soon as possible because I only had a week left of school. He told me when my week was up in school to come check in the big house, and he let me know that all the rooms that I saw when I first walked in were for employees. I felt so relieved; everything that I had been stressing about was finally taken care of. I couldn't wait until school was done. I wanted to see how my life would be completely on my own. I had to write about the good news in my diary, so when I got back to my dorm room I went straight to writing.

(Entering Diary) ...

The best is yet to come! I'm so happy. I don't know what kind of job it is, but the owner seems to be very respectful and honest. I trust the fact that he's not going to play me. Just a couple more days left of this hellhole and I'll finally be free. I would have never known this would have been the outcome when I left Virginia. I hope my mother and Moe don't find out. That would be a huge embarrassment. But then again, I'm grown now and I have to do what's best for me.

(Exiting Diary) ...

The week went by fast. I left everything that I had; I just grabbed my picture of Jazzy, my diary, and some clothes. I was ready for a new start. I left school and went straight to the strip joint. When I got there it seemed like everything was shut down, but I could hear strange noises coming from one of the girls' rooms. I walked upstairs to the owner's office so I could settle in at the owner's request. When I walked into his office, he had three gentlemen sitting there. When I walked in he was like, "Here she goes." I just stood there smiling as the men sat there staring at me. It was like they were in disbelief to see me—well, to see someone that had a body like mine. He sent me to my room, but before he closed the door completely, he told me to take a shower and change into the clothes that he had picked out for me. Once I got into my room I was so surprised by the outcome; it was better than what I'd expected. I had my own bathroom, kitchen, washer and dryer, a queen-size bed, and a TV with a stand all in the same room. It was exciting to really have my own place.

I hurried up and got dressed; I was ready for whatever was next. I mean the outfit that he wanted me to put on was something that I would have never picked out in a million years. I had no confidence in my body or even myself, and it was sad. The outfit consisted of a red tank top that showed my arms and boobs, which was showing extremely too much. I don't think I'd ever really showed my Double D's off as much until then. He also picked out some tight black shorts that were so short that I was afraid to bend over. Not only that, but there were some silver stilettos that I had no idea how to walk in. I didn't know how he knew what sizes to get, but it kind of made me feel flattered. All I kept saying to myself is, whatever it was couldn't be that bad and it's better than nothing, as Grandma Betty would always say.

When I was done, I walked back upstairs to meet the three gentlemen that were originally in his office; I was shocked to see them still there. I felt naked; I didn't want anybody to see me, not even the owner. Even though I knew he would be the one to definitely see me, whether I wanted him to or not. I stood there staring at them as they stared back at me like I was a piece of meat. I was so nervous, and at that moment I knew whatever it was couldn't be good. The owner stood up and said to me, "Let's make some money." He then walked up on the side of me and told me that the three men were my first clients and that I had to make sure I was good to them so they would come back.

I was in complete shock; I had no idea what to do or even what to say. I could have sworn having sex for money was illegal. But I soon found out that no matter what was illegal or not in New York City, anything goes. It was clearly not his first time selling a female, and it wouldn't be his last. He informed me that I was his property, and the contract stated that I would do anything that needed to be done for the club in order for him and me to be successful. I felt so dumb; why didn't I read the contract? If I'd known that I would have to sell my body to make a living, I would have never agreed to it. What did I get myself into? Once again I'd trusted a man to protect me, and I kept finding myself always back at the bottom feeling lower than dirt. I couldn't turn into that woman everyone back home would call a "ho" or "slut" while pointing and staring in disbelief. That wasn't me, and no matter how I felt about myself, I knew in the back of my mind it was wrong! At that moment I just wanted to go back home. But I knew there was no way in hell I was going home—and definitely no time soon.

11

THE UNUSUAL

He knew I was feeling some type of way because he grabbed my arm and pulled me outside of his office with so much force, I thought he was going to pull my arm right out of its socket. I broke down in tears right at that moment. He just looked at me as if he didn't have a care in the world. We stood outside of his office for five minutes as he threatened me about what would happen to me if I disobeyed him. He also let me know that it would be pointless to think I could even go to the police when they were his best-paying customers, whether it was for the strip shows or the escort services. I felt sick! I wanted to just die right then and there.

He also told me I had 10 minutes to get myself together as he walked me back to my room. I kept crying the whole way there. When we arrived at my room door, he forced me in the room and locked the door behind us. He then made me take two pills. I had no idea what they were but I took them anyways; I was petrified. He told me the pills would help me be more relaxed, and they did. It felt like I wasn't even there. That whole night went by fast; whatever he gave me truly helped me deal with the fact I had slept with three men at the same time for the first time in my life. The next morning, I woke up in so much pain, as if I'd just got hit by a moving bus. I didn't remember anything, but I knew that I did whatever it was that was required of me. There was breakfast already made for me on the counter. On the side of the plate was a note with $300 cash telling me that the boys had fun with me and they'd see me next Friday at the same time. He also wrote on the note "great job," and that there was more money from where that came from if I would just trust him; "love, Big Al" was in big letters. I stood there shaking, when I heard a knock on the door. It happened to be one of the girls that also worked there, and I was soon to find out that we had a lot of things in common.

She walked in my room and sat on my bed. I didn't know what to say; I just continued to stand there in tears. She looked as if she was 30 years old; she had a body as if she was a full-figured super-model working the runway. She introduced herself to me as Candi. She also did escort services and got tricked by Big Al in the beginning. She had recently finished up her contract but chose to stay in the big house to make more money, and she encouraged me to do the same. Especially if I had no other option. She told me she would show me the ropes, and be there for me if I needed anything or anyone to talk to. I broke down even more! Literally falling down on the floor, feeling so ashamed. But I knew I was too deep into it for me to back out. She sat right beside me, consoling me as she shed tears herself. Even though she was starting to get used to the life that she was living, she still felt ashamed and wanted better for herself. The moment we shared kind of taught me a lesson. She also let me know that the pills Big Al gave me were E pills, and that it was best for me to take them with a shot of some type of alcohol to ease any pain before dealing with the low-down dirty dogs.

I took all the advice Candi gave me. Before I knew it months went by, and I was turning into someone I'd never thought I would become. I turned into a drug, alcohol, sex addict addicted to the money. I forgot about everything else in my life, and I thank Candi for that. She was like a big sister to me, and she helped me in ways you would only imagine.

I loved all the attention I was getting from the men; it made me feel like I was important and loved. But I can say that I never had clients on a Sunday as respect for the Lord. I informed Big Al that if he wanted me to be one of his girls, he would have to respect the fact that Sundays didn't work for me. I mean I wasn't the religious type, but I knew in my heart that there was a God that watched over me each and every day, even though I was in a bunch of mess. Candi and I were so close that we even did private parties together, went shopping together, and everything else you could think of. We even decided that when we both raised up enough money, we would get out of this type of lifestyle we were in and own our very own soul-food restaurant. Candi was a banging cook. But as usual things don't always go as planned!

On a regular day like any other day in the business, something traumatized me forever. It was on a Sunday night at the big house. I was coming back in from being out that whole day shopping; I was enjoying my day off. Candi and I were going out clubbing that night, but she had to take care of her clients for the day first. I was walking to my room to get dressed and ready when I heard someone screaming from one of the rooms. I didn't know who it was, but something in me told me to walk down the hall to Candi's room. When I walked into Candi's room, she was being raped and beaten by two white men. I dropped everything and ran to her rescue. I fought them as hard as I could, but when it was all said and done the damage was already done to me and Candi. We had black eyes, busted lips; Candi even had a chipped tooth. It was crazy because the strip joint was covered with security, but this time no one was in sight. I felt bad because someone else I knew had gone through what I did, and I knew exactly how she felt. At that moment we both decided enough was enough, so we grabbed everything we had and ran. But we still weren't done with the lifestyle that would ultimately kill us. Sex, money, and drugs were all we knew. But we had to survive, and the real survival now had to be done throughout the streets.

12

DRAINED

We didn't know really what to do. We both had no other work experiences other than giving sexual favors. We walked around the city streets the whole night, not making a single dime. We realized getting some good clientele was going to be harder than what we'd thought. So we just checked into a hotel in Queens for the night; we were too drained to keep moving forward. When we finally got into our hotel room, we were down for the count. But we knew that we were determined to get money no matter what, so the next morning we got up and went right back into the crazy world.

The next morning when we were walking the streets of New York City, we happened to find someone that had connections with the underground and knew exactly the perfect spot for us to do our business. In other words, the track where prostitutes worked. So later on that night we went to the location and did what we did best. In the same night we came back with hundreds of dollars, along with all different types of drugs. Candi and I always had little parties between us before and after we did what we did. We were all about the money and nothing else mattered. Something that was supposed to be temporary for us to get on our feet turned into something that we were doing for years. The only thing we did about our living situation was move into a better hotel. It was more comfortable for us to do that than to get an apartment. In those years, we went through a whole lot of mess that no one would ever understand. We did something that we didn't want to do; and that was get addicted to the lifestyle.

There was no way out; we took life as it was and everything else just fell into place. We even got locked up from time to time for prostitution and drug possession, but that didn't stop us. We couldn't stop; it was clear we were going to die in these streets—well at least one of us. On July 26, 1996 on a Friday night, we went on the track to do what we do. But when we got there, it was like we were the only females out, which was very unusual. In all these years there were always other females that we had to compete with. It should have been a sign to turn back around and go back to the hotel, but we didn't. We just grinded even harder. As time went on a black sedan pulled up on us; we thought whoever was in the car would be the one to give us the big bucks. But when he pulled up on us, he put a gun in our faces and forced us to get in the car. When we got in the car, we realized that there were two other men in the backseat. They took us to an abandoned building and raped us.

We yelled and screamed but no one could hear us. When they were done they informed us that they would be our pimps from now on, and we couldn't be out on the streets without them or there would be consequences. Candi and I refused, so they ended up beating us so bad that we could barely move. When they were done doing what they did to us, they put us right back on the corner and sat in an alley down the street watching us. Ten minutes after standing there, we decided to make a run for it. They began to chase and shoot at us. Seconds later after they began shooting at us, one of the bullets hit Candi right in her back and killed her instantly. I was next; but cops were coming because they heard the gunshots. So they ended up driving off in the opposite direction. I had no other choice but to leave Candi's dead body at the scene. I didn't know what to do; I ended up running back to the hotel. When I got back to the hotel room, I cried my eyes out. I sat there in our hotel room watching the news. I couldn't believe Candi was dead. I then turned around and did something that I hadn't done in years, and that was to write in my diary.

13

REHAB

(Entering Diary) ...

Why? What did we do, Lord, that was so horrible that you had to take Candi's life? After we just went through that torture. (Tears flowing.) I'm so sick of this; why does life have to be this way? I just want to be loved, but most of all I just want to be happy. I messed up big time; I need a change! Why every time I get close to someone, you always take them away from me? I don't want to be alone! I'm so tired; take me! Why won't you just take me!

(Exiting Diary) ...

After I was done writing in my diary, I just cried myself to sleep. I couldn't take it. Another one of my friends was dead and gone, and there was nothing I could do about it. I was back to square one having no one but myself. Those next few days I didn't go on the track; I was too afraid to go back on the streets. Life took a whole new twist and turn. I started thinking more and more about my mom, Jazzy, and even

---

Moe. It had been years since I'd seen or heard from them. I wanted to go home at that moment but was unsure if I even had a home. But then again I didn't want my mother seeing me like this—or anyone from back home, for that matter. I told myself I needed help. So I decided to check myself into a rehab to get cleaned up. On August 9, 1996, I decided to check into Sunnyside Rehabilitation Center in the Bronx. I was so scared; I didn't know if I was going to truly get the help I needed or not, but I knew I had to do something.

Rehab was the hardest thing for me. I didn't want to deal with the fact that I'd had a problem all these years. When I first went to the rehab site, I was unaware of the fact that I had to stay in the facility in order to get cleaned up. I had to make the sacrifice and stay, even though I hated the fact that I had to. I was in rehab for six months fighting off so many addictions. It was the longest six months of my life. The process was the worst; I went through millions of withdrawals. They even had to stop me a few times from walking out; I was fed up. But I thank God for them because if they hadn't stopped me from reentering the cold streets of New York City, I don't know where I would be right now. They really care about their patients and their well-being. Rehab showed me how to love and respect myself, but most of all to know my worth. Our group meetings every week were very inspirational; they gave us knowledge on how to move forward on the right paths in life.

Listening to former drug addicts, pimps, drug dealers, prostitutes, and alcoholics talk about their lives and how they overcame really helped. I think I was the biggest cry-baby of the group because I always cried during our group sessions. During my time in rehab there was a sweet older woman named Ms. Harrington, who was one of the counselors that stuck by me the whole time praying for me. She was truly a woman of God. I knew there were people in the world like her, and I'm grateful for every moment that we shared. After the completion of rehab, they helped you get a job and a place so you could remain humble as you went back into the world as a new human being. I was ready for my new beginning, and I knew that this was my second chance from God. There was no way in hell I was looking backwards, but I was simply moving forward.

At first I was a little nervous about the job search. I didn't think anyone would want to hire a former prostitute. But Ms. Harrington would always tell me to have faith because something would come through. Ms. Harrington was a strong believer of the word of God, so whatever Ms. Harrington told me I normally believed; I knew God was definitely in her corner.

14

FORGIVENESS

Wow, I can't believe I'm 24 and having to literally restart my life all over again. All because of the bad choices and mistakes I've made. I'm determined to get myself together, and no one or anything is going to get in my way this time. I had literally four weeks left of rehab, and it was time for me to finally look at my new apartment in Manhattan. Would you believe out of everywhere I've been in the city, Manhattan was the most peaceful of them all to me? It was an apartment in a complex that had a beautiful view of Times Square from a distance; it was a little small but it worked. On top of that, the center furnished my whole apartment so I didn't have to worry about that issue. I cried when Ms. Harrington gave me my keys to my new place and told me I could move in the same day. The day she handed me my keys, she also told me that she would love for me to go to church with her one Sunday, even though it was against the center policy to ask a patient to go anywhere personal. Without any hesitation I told her yes. I knew there was something bigger and better out there, and the Lord's house would give me just the clarity I needed.

After we left my apartment, Ms. Harrington took me to a few job interviews; none of them was for me. I couldn't really see myself working in the fast-food business, but I just went with the flow. I couldn't wait until we were done with those job interviews so I could go home and write in my diary. The next day Ms. Harrington and I were back to square one looking for jobs—well, interviews that we could attend right on the spot. There was one job that did interest me, and the pay wasn't bad either. But when we got there everyone had already left and gone home. I thought Fridays were when people stayed at work the latest, but I guess not. Or maybe it was just my line of work that always made me stay out late. After a while, Ms. Harrington and I decided to just call it a day and pick up on everything on Monday.

That night I stayed in my apartment. I sat up all night thinking about everything I had gone through, and how I'd made it out by the skin of my teeth. By seven-something in the morning, I was finally falling asleep when there was a knock on the door. I was nervous and scared to even go to the door. I hadn't been living there long enough to really be getting any visitors. I was happy when I looked through the peek-hole and saw Ms. Harrington standing there. I immediately opened the door. She'd stopped by to make sure I was okay and to see if I needed anything. She had a Bible and a plate in her hand as she walked through the door. I couldn't really tell what she'd brought, but whatever it was smelled so good. She sat down on my couch and handed me the Bible and plate. Out of my entire life I'd never held a Bible in my hand, and it was sad. Ms. Harrington always had some encouraging words to say. She also came to remind me about church Sunday morning, and that she would be there at 10 am to get me so I needed to be ready. I just said okay; but inside I was really excited about going, because I didn't know what to expect. Ms. Harrington left soon after that. I could tell she knew I hadn't slept and she was just being respectful like she'd always been.

Sunday morning came fast; I had no idea what to wear for church, but all I knew was that I just wanted Ms. Harrington to be pleased. Ms. Harrington came right on time, and she was happier than ever to see me. She told me that she felt in her heart that this was the day the Lord would really show up in my life. I believed her as always, especially when it had to do with God. We went to Mount Calvary Baptist Church in Manhattan that morning. The church was a little small, but I realized size didn't matter. As we were walking inside of the church, I found out that I wasn't the only one that respected Ms. Harrington; the whole congregation did. People were very nice; it gave me a feeling that I'd never felt before. It was like they cared without even knowing me or the things I went through, and I needed that right at that moment, being that I still felt broken inside. Before the pastor went up to the pulpit, Ms. Harrington introduced me to him. His name was Alfred Bentley Sr. I couldn't believe that the same man that was walking through the track years ago trying to get women off the streets would really be a pastor. We used to think he was just this crazy man that was pretending. When he first saw me it was clear that he remembered me; his words were "praise God" and "God is so good." I broke down right at that moment, because I knew exactly what he was praising God for. Ms. Harrington just consoled me while the pastor stood there and prayed for me. I finally felt free. When everything was all said and done, Ms. Harrington and I sat back down to get ready for the service. Even though I felt like I'd already got what I came for. But I found out there was more that God had in store for me. I sat there the whole service in tears;

I was too overwhelmed. Ms. Harrington continued to do what she always did best, and that was praising and giving God the glory.

Before the service was done, Pastor Bentley called an altar call for people that wanted to be forgiven, delivered, have a new start, or just needed and wanted God. At first I was hesitating; it was clear that the altar was something important and a personal choice. But I ended up going to the altar eventually. I knew I needed a new start, but most of all I wanted it. Ms. Harrington didn't walk me up there, but I could hear her still praising him in the background. As soon as I got to the altar, I broke down asking God to forgive me for everything I'd done. I felt so ashamed. I knew I needed help from God, and I definitely wanted it. When I left the altar, I could hear all the saints in the sanctuary praising God while repeatedly saying "it has been done." "Done" meaning all my worries were no longer there. God now had me, and all I had to do was trust and believe in him. At that moment I knew my life would be changed forever.

I felt refreshed. God cleaned me up and allowed me to realize I had everything to live for. I surrendered myself and gave God me. I was happy and felt good about myself; I was finally free of all my sins. After the service was over, I went to Pastor Bentley personally and thanked him for everything; but most of all for doing God's will. He gave me some encouraging words: to read my Bible and to stay prayed up, and God would do the rest. I let him know that I was so grateful! I wanted to do whatever it was that the Lord needed me to do. That same day I became a member of the church. When Ms. Harrington and I left the church, I couldn't stop smiling from ear to ear and telling God "thank you." To celebrate, Ms. Harrington and I went out to eat. At the restaurant we continued to praise God for all that he had done. After we were done eating, I went home to my new place and Ms. Harrington went back to the center for her shift. The next day was a big day for me, so I just went home and wrote in my diary and got ready for bed, feeling brand new.

15

THE FUTURE CALLS

The next morning, I woke up feeling like a new me, and I loved every minute of it. After I got dressed, I sat on my couch and began to read my Bible for the first time. All I could say was "wow," because it gave me a revelation of who God is, eternal life, and what happens if we disobeyed him. But most of all, that God himself loves me with an everlasting love. I knew at that moment life was real and there was no turning back. So I decided and declared to myself I would do things that only pleased God. I trusted God so much that I knew that I was going to get the job of my dreams. I knew whatever I wanted in Jesus Christ's name, I could have. I was finally one with my real Father.

Ms. Harrington came around 8 o'clock in the morning to get me. Every time I saw her, she always had this glow about her. She was truly a blessed woman. We had three job interviews back to back; they all were data-entry positions. They were actually the kind of jobs I wanted. Two of the interviews didn't go so well because I didn't have enough experience. But Ms. Harrington and I still had faith that something would come through. The last interview was at a dental office. It was a family-owned business that was connected to a house. When I walked into the office, Ms. Harrington knew a lot of the people working there. My new pastor and his son were the owners of the business and his son was the hirer; that made me even more nervous. I had no idea what to say. I waited in the lobby to be interviewed for about five minutes, shaking.

When it was finally time to be interviewed, he took me to the back where his office was and told me to have a seat in one of the chairs that was there. The interview process lasted for about an hour of us just talking about every-thing—well, God. His name was also David Bentley; he was my age and was the assistant pastor at the church. He was so pleased with how I answered my interview questions that I got the job right on the spot. I was so happy. He in-formed me that I had to come back the next day for orienta-tion before Ms. Harrington and I left. I was emotional about everything; as soon as we got in the car, I couldn't help but break down in tears. I couldn't believe how far I had truly come. God is truly a good God.

Ms. Harrington just sat there in the car with me praising God while I continued crying my eyes out; she was very un-derstanding. When we finally left from in front of the dental office, Ms. Harrington dropped me off at home so I could rest and get ready for my new job in the morning. I was so excited that I couldn't sleep. I sat up reading my Bible and thanking God for everything he had done for me. I ended up reading my Bible for hours. But before I went to bed, I made sure I wrote about the exciting news in my diary.

(Entering Diary) ...

I never thought I would be at this point in my life. But I'm happy I'm here. I can't thank God enough for everything that he has done for me. But I learned over the years to just take everything day by day. I'm truly blessed! I would say I'm a little nervous, though, about work tomorrow, but I know that God didn't bring me this far to leave me high and dry. So I know everything will be all right. Plus, I'm ready more than ever to see what my future holds!

(Exiting Diary) ...

16

THE PAST MUST STAY IN THE PAST

woke up feeling refreshed! My life started to take a whole new toll on me. I deserved to be happy. Before I could do anything, I continued to read my Bible. I knew it would be just the start I needed for what lay ahead. I was still a little nervous about starting my new job, though; but I was right there on time to do whatever I needed to do for it to be a success. I was the receptionist for the whole office. David was such a nice person; whenever I needed anything he was right there. Even at the office they would get together and have prayer meetings; because of that I was getting stronger in God and his word. As time went on, I could tell that David had a little thing for me. But he was so respectful, he didn't even know how to express himself. But in a way I was happy he didn't; I wasn't ready for any kind of relationship if it wasn't with God. There was only one man at the time that had my mind, body, and soul; and that was the almighty God himself.

Even at church he would act a little shy; to be honest, that's the first place I realized his interest. But one day David got the courage to ask me out to dinner; I didn't really know what to say. I mean I didn't want to, and it wasn't because

I wasn't interested, but that I was scared of getting hurt again. Eventually I did end up saying yes, just to see where his head was. His head was right in the right place, and doing the will of God. God was surely using him in a mighty way; he was an excellent minister at our church that knew how to touch God's people in such a special way. Our first date was at a nice fancy restaurant that was in the middle of nowhere. I loved every minute of it; it was definitely something new. At the restaurant I had the best time talking, laughing, and gazing into his beautiful hazel eyes; it was so amazing. After dinner he took me home, but he made sure he asked me out on a second date before I got out of the car. I said "No"; I didn't really want to take the chance. But in my heart I knew he wasn't that type of guy.

The next day I didn't want to go to work. I felt like it was going to be a lot of tension from both of us. But I still left and went anyways. When I got there, David was nowhere to be found. He had taken the day off. I felt bad; I thought it was because of me that he didn't show up for work. Around 4 o'clock, an hour before the office was about to close, David came walking in the doors. I was shocked to see him and happy at the same time. When he walked in everything was still the same between us, like last night didn't even happen. He said hi to everyone in the office and came right back to the reception desk to talk to me. He wanted to take me out again so bad and he wasn't taking no for an answer. I kept saying that I couldn't, it wasn't the right time for me; but he kept being consistent. So once again on a Sunday after church, he took me to dinner. He wanted to know why I wasn't interested and if I wanted him to just leave me alone completely. In my whole entire life, I'd never had a man chase me—well they didn't have to. I was always an easy target in the past for men to take advantage of. At that moment, I knew he was very sincere and I needed someone in my life in general that was like that.

So I apologized to him for the way I was treating him; he was very understanding. That night at dinner was very special, just like our first date. We both shared things with each other that were dear to our hearts. But most of all, I was shocked when he told me that his mother died when he was only three years old to breast cancer. That situation brought tears to my eyes. I could relate because my best friend had also died of cancer. The fact that I hadn't seen my mother in years also hurt me; I had no idea where she was. It hurt me inside, and I could tell that David noticed that. When we were done eating, David took me to get some ice cream to cheer me up. We had a lot in common; we even liked the same kind of ice cream. That same night I tried to invite him into my apartment so we could talk more, but he declined my invitation. He saw the look on my face and went straight to explaining himself and why he couldn't. He let me know that he really liked me and didn't want to do anything that would mess that up. Not only that, but as a man of God he didn't want to overstep his boundaries by going inside my home, and I respected that. He made me feel good. No man had ever respected me in that way.

I was excited; he gave me just the confidence that I needed to trust again. When I got in the house, I said my prayers and went straight to bed. I couldn't wait for work in the morning. The next day at work was a little weird; it was like the spotlight was on us—everyone was starting to see that we both liked each other and were getting closer by the minute. It seemed like every night he was taking me out to dinner. He loved to feed me. I was big enough and didn't need any extra baggage. But he loved everything about me, even my flaws. We went out to dinner—or should I say on dates? —millions of times before he even got the courage to ask me to be his girlfriend; well, more than that. But when he did it was something special.

I remember it like it was yesterday; it was on April 27, Easter Sunday—and what a beautiful Sunday that was. Praise and worship was about to begin when the pastor announced to the congregation that David had a special announcement; no one had any idea what was coming next. He went into talking about how God had blessed him over the past few months, and because of God he had met a wonderful person. I was clueless; and so was everyone else. He then said four magical words that I'd never thought I would ever hear in a million years—well not for me anyways. "Will you marry me?" He was something special; I knew he was the one for me, and it felt good that he wanted me to be the one for him. So I said yes and felt really good about it. My dreams were finally coming true. But that's when reality hit me: how could I get married without my mom at least being there?

Even in My Mess

- *Lord, even in my mess I know you're able...*
- *I know your love is and will always be an everlasting love...*
- *Even in my mess, I knew there was something greater and I knew it was you...*
- *Time may pass me by, but I know your word will always remain true...*
- *Even in my mess, I realized faith is what keeps me...*
- *Even in my mess, you wipe away my tears...*
- *Even when my heart is heavy, I know you hold me close and remove my burdens*

- *Trials and tribulations may come my way, but victory is still mine...*
- *The devil is and will always be a liar; I am who you say I am, and because of that I am forever grateful...*

Your one and only,
Destiny Jones

17

TIME WAITS FOR NO ONE

I was so overwhelmed, but happy at the same time. Everything that I'd ever wanted in life was finally coming true. After church service was over David and I, along with Pastor Bentley and Ms. Harrington, went out to dinner to talk more about the future wedding that was soon to come. At the restaurant, I expressed my feelings about the whole wedding and how I needed my mother to be there. I couldn't see myself having a big wedding without her, or at least letting her know about it. They were very understanding about the whole thing, and encouraged me to go back home to Virginia. When dinner was over Ms. Harrington and Pastor Bentley went their own separate ways, while David and I went back to my place and talked over our upcoming event more. David expressed to me that he wanted to get married as soon as possible; and so did I. He also let me know that he was going with me to Virginia for support. I was happy and relieved! Sometimes David was too good to be true. After we were done talking about the situation, David left and went home, while I sat up the entire night praying, reading my Bible, and writing in my diary! I was so scared about reconnecting with my mother. I had no idea what to say to her, or even what she would say to me; but all I knew was that it had to be done.

(Entering Diary) ...

Sighs... Wow... I never dreamed that this would ever happen to me. I'm getting married! To a man that loves and respects me for me. He is truly the man of my dreams. I can't wait until we make it official! I always wanted a family of my own, and I'm happy that I'm going to have that with David. I know he will be a great husband, but most of all a great father when the time comes. I can't believe I'm even thinking about kids; my life has truly changed. I want my mother to be part of this so bad. I love my mother and always will, even though I haven't seen or heard from her in years. I love the fact that David understood my hurt and pain over my mother's situation, and is willing to support me in any way possible. I know my mother will love him. God is truly doing some great things in my life.

(Exiting Diary) ...

The next day I woke up ready to do what was needed to be done. I got on the phone and called my mother for the first time in years. No one answered the phone but I knew it was still her phone number, as I heard her voice on the answering machine. She sounded so beautiful and happy; I missed her like crazy. I broke down in tears just from hearing her voice. I didn't leave a message—I couldn't figure out what to really say. When I got to work, I pulled David over to the side to tell him about the call I made to my mother. David encouraged me to keep calling until I could reach her; and I did. I really needed to talk to her. When I tried calling the second time I got the same result: no answer. But that time I left a message on the phone, letting her know that it was me, and I was getting married soon and wanted to come home so we could see each other. I felt good after I left the message. But she didn't call me back the same day or any other day.

Weeks went by and there was still no response from her. I felt so hurt! How could my own mother be so cruel, and not want anything to do with her own child? David and I were so ready to get married that we ended up just going to city hall. I couldn't see myself having a big wedding without her being there to share that happy moment with me. After David and I got married, we bought a house in Long Island. We felt it was the best place to raise a family. Even though my life seemed to be going well, David could still see that I was incomplete without my mother's presence. So he ended up surprising me with a trip to Virginia for a week. When we got to Virginia, everything was so different. There were things built that I'd never seen before, and places that were knocked down that once meant so much to me growing up. I felt sick to my stomach with all the changes that took place. The first day was very challenging for me. I kept throwing up, feeling dizzy and very lightheaded. David couldn't take me being in so much pain, so he suggested that I go to the hospital to get checked out.

At the hospital in the waiting room I ran into Jazzy's mother, Ms. Gloria, who was now a nurse at the hospital. As soon as she saw me, she ran up to me and gave me a big hug and kiss. I was so shocked to see her, but happy at the same time to see that she was doing well. I introduced her to David and informed her that I still lived in New York, and that now I was also married. She was so happy for me. She even broke down in tears, telling me that she missed me and wished that I could come back home to visit more often. She told me that my mother had been heartbroken over the years, because she had no idea where I was or even if I was okay. I broke down in tears right at that moment, because here I was thinking that my mother didn't care about me. When in all reality she had been looking for me and hurting all these years, just like I was.

I felt bad; I never knew that my mother was hurting because of me. I needed to see her! I asked Ms. Gloria if she knew where my mother was, and she informed me that my mother had left Moe years ago and was now married to a man named Steve. Not only that, but I had a baby brother who was now four years old. I was completely shocked and overwhelmed by the whole conversation. I couldn't believe that I had a baby brother and a stepfather at the same time. She also let me know that my mother had moved out of Grandma Betty's home and also changed her number. Everything was starting to make sense. I just knew my mother couldn't be that coldhearted. Before I could get and write down her new address, the doctor called for me. When we got into one of the rooms, the doctor let me and David know exactly what was going on. I was three weeks pregnant. My mouth just dropped; I couldn't believe I was going to be a mother. When I looked over at David he had a smile on his face; he'd always wanted to be a father and his dreams were finally coming true. Everything was happening so fast; we had only been married for a month, not even.

When we left the room and walked back to the front to check-out, I pulled Ms. Gloria to the side to tell her the good news. I let her know that it was even more important now to find my mother, being that she was going to be a grandmother. She congratulated me and gave me the address. When David and I left the hospital we went straight over to the house. I was so scared; I couldn't get out of the car. David encouraged me and let me know that he would be right there with me the whole time; which he was. We were in the car for about 15 minutes before I got the courage to get out and knock on the door. The house was so beautiful; I haven't even met the man that was my mother husband, but from what I seen on the outside my mother was a lucky woman. As I was knocking on the door I could hear a little boy call for his mother. I got so emotional. Seconds later my mother came to the door; and when she seen it was me she broke down in tears, and so did I. she just took me into her arms as she whispered to me that she would never let us be apart again. I couldn't say anything; tears just kept flowing.

Moments later a guy and a child came to the door. It was her husband Steve carrying my little brother Steven. It was like they knew all about me; my little brother came up to me and said hi sissy. It was the best feeling ever when I found out I was a big sister. After everyone sat down in the living room, my mother and I talked about everything that had been going on in our lives the past few years. She was disappointed with the terrible things that occurred; but was happy that I was finally happy. When I told her that I was married and pregnant she broke down again in tears. But I can say that every tear my mother and I shared was happy tears, because we were finally reunited and living lives we always dreamed.

18

REUNITED

It felt so good to finally be reunited with my mother. Without her I was incomplete. They say you only get one and once she's gone that's it. So from that day forward I cherished her. I missed enough time already, and wasn't going to miss anymore. She was still beautiful as ever and her smile still brighten up any room. She had this beautiful glow about her. I could definitely see how happy she was. God is good even far and near. But time surely waits on no one.

After we sat in my mother's living room talking for hours drinking tea. We all went out to dinner as one big happy family. My baby brother was so adorable; we looked so much alike. He was a split image of me when I was his age just a tap bit lighter. We sat at the restaurant talking about future goals that we all had. My mother and Steve even informed David and me that they were planning on moving up to New York in the next year or two, but just wanted to make sure all their affairs were in order. Steve was originally from New Orleans and moved to Virginia a few years ago due to the fact his mother was ill. A few weeks after he moved to Virginia, she ended up dying. But before she died, she informed him that she was having dreams about him settling down having a family of his own, and that his future was right here in Virginia. Two weeks after his mother's death, he met my mother at a little coffee shop down the road from Grandma Betty's house. They immediately fell head over heels for each other. And two weeks prior to that, my mother finally left Moe. They were definitely destined to be together, just like David and I.

Steve owned three soul-food restaurants that were making a killing. He ended up owning one in Virginia, New Orleans, and Atlanta. But he ended up getting rid of the Atlanta restaurant when they had my baby brother so he could be there more for his family. Both restaurants were called "Hope and Food for the Soul." Their restaurant was so beautiful! David and I had no idea the restaurant that we were sitting in was actually theirs. It was definitely an upscale restaurant. I felt so special sitting there. The food was so delicious; I knew for sure my mother's touch was in it. I could remember her southern cooking like it was yesterday. I was finally happy to say that I had a family. At the dinner table, my mother even informed me of what actually went down between her and Moe. I didn't really care; I was just happy she was out of the picture. But I still listened! Moe ended up cheating on her with this white lady three houses down from where we used to live. The lady ended up moving on the block right after I went off to college. Not only that but she started hanging out with the wrong crowd, and my mother simply wasn't having it. She also ended up confessing that their relationship was only supposed to be something short term that just ended up being much more because she was vulnerable at the time. I had so much more respect for my mother after that night due to the fact she kept it 100% honest with me. She told me things that I never thought I would know. I was happy she was finally happy.

I mean in the beginning I was not too sure about my stepfather at first, but he ended up growing on me. I could see that he really loved my mother and little brother; not only that, but he was willing to accept me as his very own. I mean it shouldn't really matter whether or not we got along, but we did. She was my mother way before she was his wife, so it would only be right that he respected me and I respected him. After dinner and dessert, David and I went back to our hotel room and went to sleep. My mother and stepfather wanted us to stay in their guest room but we refused; we wanted them to have their privacy and we wanted ours. The next morning, I woke up with a smile on my face. I felt like I did the day that David and I got married. I felt like everything was becoming complete. But there was still one thing that I had to do that I wasn't really ready to come to reality with, and that was visiting Jazzy.

19

MEMORIES

After our lunch date, David and I went to the gravesite where my once best friend now lay. I had butterflies the whole ride there. I was so nervous; I didn't know what to say or do. I hadn't talked or seen her in years, and I knew that it would be more years to come without her. I missed her so much! Life would have been so much different if she were still alive. I know if she were still around, she would have been so disappointed in me and the things I'd done, but at the same time happy with the fact I got myself together. I wish Jazzy and David could have met each other. Jazzy was a very respectable person who wasn't the type to judge anyone, even when I did. She is truly indeed my guardian angel. She always got me out of trouble no matter what the situation was. I still can't believe she's gone!

Even though David didn't know Jazzy, he still went with me to the cemetery for support. Her gravesite was just around the corner from our old middle school where we first met. I broke down immediately. David had to damn near carry me over to where she was resting. I took it as hard as I did when she first passed away. I couldn't believe I was standing over my once best friend's gravestone. It was just a reality that she was gone and never coming back! As I stood there shaking and telling her how much I missed and loved her, David kept whispering in my ear that everything was going to be okay, and that God never gives us too much that we can't handle. In my heart I knew it was a part of God's plan, but I just didn't understand why it had to be my best friend.

I sat there shedding tears over my once best friend for 15 minutes before I could get any other words out. But I knew that I wasn't leaving until I let her know exactly how I felt. Even though I already knew she knew how I felt. That day truly changed me. It helped me overcome and deal more with the fact that she was no longer there physically but in spirit. When we left the cemetery, we went back to my mother's house and enjoyed some more time with them. When I got to my mother's house, I told her that I was coming from seeing Jazzy, and she informed me that she visited Jazzy every Sunday. I was so surprised; my mother hated cemeteries. She said she would go to Jazzy and pray that she watched over me while I was out there in this crazy world; and she did. Thank God for his grace and mercy. David and my stepfather went out back and talked while my mother and I sat in the kitchen drinking tea, reminiscing about all the good times that we'd both shared with Jazzy. She was definitely a blessing! I'm just happy that Momma Gloria found a way to live without her baby girl.

My mother had changed so much since the last time I saw her. But then again so had I. We both had this type of maturity about us. Even though we'd both been through hell and back, victory was surely ours and we definitely claimed it! I never thought my mother and I's relationship would have ever gotten back to the way it was, but I'm happy we're reunited and moving forward. I always dreamed of being someone's sister, and I'm happy that has definitely come to pass. I mean Jazzy was my sister and I treated her like we were sisters. But Jazzy was no longer here, and it felt different knowing someone out there came from the same woman I came from and shared the same blood. If anything was to ever happen, he would have me and I would have him. If my mother would have stayed with Moe, I don't know how the outcome would have been. But as my husband said everything happens for a reason, and thank God she was able to get out of that toxic relationship.

My mother now has a life that she always dreamed of. I'm so happy she finally got herself together and got over those lames in her past. Steve was definitely her Prince Charming. Growing up I thought she would never get over my father, but to God be the glory! I can't thank him enough. I used to think everything was my father's fault, but it actually wasn't. I don't know where he's at or even if he's still alive. One day, God willing, we too will be reunited and able to rekindle something. Only time will tell!

20

BLESSED

I'm so happy that I finally reunited with my mother. It felt good to know that she was still there in Virginia and happy. That week vacation was definitely needed; thank God for my husband. David and I went back home feeling really good about everything that had taken place. We couldn't wait to go back to visit. Life for us seemed to be getting better by the minute. On our vacation, we were blessed with the news that we were having a baby and couldn't wait to tell Pastor Bentley and Ms. Harrington.

When we got back, David immediately called his father and I called Ms. Harrington. We couldn't wait until Sunday to tell them the good news. We knew that they would be just as excited as we were. Come to find out Pastor Bentley and Ms. Harrington were together having dinner. When they were done having dinner, they ran to our house and embraced us. It felt so good to be back home. I loved seeing my mother, but I couldn't see my life without Ms. Harrington; I missed her! She was truly a woman of God and a blessing. The four of us sat around in the living room with tears of Joy. David and I not only told them about the baby but about everything else that happened while we were in Virginia. They were happy that I was finally able to reunite with my family and wished to meet them one day. It felt like we hadn't seen them in years. We sat up talking for hours. We even prayed together as a family for not only our new beginnings but for my unborn child.

I couldn't thank God enough for blessing me with everything that I could only imagine. Who said there were no such things as miracles! Life for us went back to normal. We were so excited that the first week after finding out we were having a baby, we immediately started setting up the nursery. Everyone from the church was blessing us with gifts. "Grateful" wasn't the word! God was definitely a God of love, and he blessed me more than I could imagine. It didn't matter to me if the baby was a boy or girl; I just wanted a healthy baby. David, on the other hand, wanted a girl. He'd always read books and seen movies with a father-and-daughter relationship and always wanted his own daddy's little girl. But at the same time, we both told ourselves that we would be satisfied with whatever the Lord blessed us with, because no matter what we were going to be the best parents we could be.

My mother was so happy she was going to be a grandmother. We talked on the phone every day, and she even came up once to visit so far. She already had a nickname for the baby. No matter what, the baby was her "stinky butt." It was too cute to see how excited my mother was. I just knew that my baby was going to be a blessed baby. So many people were patiently waiting for the arrival. David insisted on the baby being named after him, whether it was a girl or boy. I totally disagreed; I think that was the only time David and I disagreed on something. David the 3rd or David were just not names I wanted to pick. When I think about it I begin to laugh.

To me my pregnancy was going by fast and smoothly. Before I knew it I was five months pregnant, carrying a real live baby inside of me. David cried the first time he felt the baby kick. He couldn't believe what he was experiencing. We both were anxiously waiting. When it was time for my annual checkup, we were so excited. We were finally going to find out what we were having. We ended up finding out that we were having a baby girl. David cried his eyes out. He'd always wanted a daddy's little girl, and that's just what he was going to get! We were so happy that I felt like dancing for the Lord right then and there. But while we were extremely happy, the doctor had an unsure look on his face that ended up bringing us from 1,000 back down to reality. Before we knew it, we were hit with some bad news.

21

IN GOD WE TRUST

The doctor informed us with the news that possibly, I would not be able to carry the baby full term. My uterus wasn't strong enough to hold her; and if I did carry her to full term, it would not only be a miracle but impossible for us both to come out alive. I immediately thought of my past. Could my past experiences of being beaten and raped have caused my body to reject my Baby!?! David and I were confused! We couldn't understand why this was happening to us. All over again I felt like my whole world was crashing down on me.

After we left the doctor's office, I broke down in the parking lot. I was no longer crying tears of joy but tears of hurt, confusion, and sadness. I called and told my mother as soon as I got home what was going on. I didn't know what to do or even where to turn, but I knew my mother would say something that would keep me calm for the moment. When she picked up the phone, she immediately knew something wasn't right. She told me that everything would be all right and to just trust in God. I couldn't believe that I was getting all worked up by what the doctor had said when the only one that has the last say is God. I immediately stopped all my crying and feeling sorry for myself and went straight to praying. God was the one that could save me and my baby. From that day forward David and I looked to the hills from which came our help, and our help came from the Lord. We focused on the fact that God had everything under control. For my whole pregnancy my doctor kept trying to give our daughter an expiration date, but David and I just kept praying that God's will would be done.

There was nothing too hard for God! I was so comfortable during my pregnancy; I had a great support system. When I got the news that the baby and I were at risk, David and Ms. Harrington ordered me not to work anymore. They took care of everything so I didn't have to worry about anything. I ended up not being able to travel anymore back and forth to Virginia, but I was happy and blessed that my mother came up once a month to check on me; even Momma Gloria came up a few times. My little brother was patiently waiting for his baby niece's arrival, and so was I. I couldn't wait until the nightmare was over. But I knew no matter what for me and my house, we were going to trust the Lord all the way through.

Before I knew it I was nine months pregnant, ready to master what the devil thought he could destroy. God was too good to me! When my water finally broke, I was anxious but nervous at the same time. At that moment I knew it was time to trust God more than I ever had, and to prove all the doubters and naysayers just how mighty my God truly is! At the end of the day, my family knew the outcome already. I cried all the way to the hospital. My emotions were all over the place. Those past nine months felt like eternity, and now it was finally coming to an end.

22

GOD'S STILL IN CONTROL

When David and I arrived at the hospital, my doctor immediately wanted to rush me to surgery. I was having an emergency C-section. I was so surprised to see my mother and Momma Gloria already there waiting in the waiting room. My mother and Momma Gloria had no idea I was having my baby that day, but they'd already had plans to come to New York to surprise me. I definitely wasn't expecting them but I was glad they were there; even Ms. Harrington ended up showing up before I was rushed to surgery. I was so happy, tears just kept flowing down my cheeks. We all held hands and prayed together as a family before it was time for me to finally deliver.

As the doctor began to operate on me, my heart rate dropped; I started to panic! I couldn't believe I was acting like Peter, one of Jesus' disciples. Peter trusted Jesus so much that he jumped in the middle of the sea; and like Peter I took my eyes off of Jesus and I began to sink. But just like in the Bible, Jesus came to Peters' rescue. So I immediately knew I had to continue to be focused on him, who would also save me just like he saved Peter. The whole delivery was a constant battle. I was beginning to lose a lot of blood so the doctor wanted to stop, but that would have meant my baby girl would have died. I couldn't allow that to happen!

I informed my doctor that no matter what happened I needed him to save my baby. Tears flowed from David and me as we prayed and prayed the whole way through. David had this look in his eyes that showed he was trusting in God, and I knew that whatever happened our family would come out victorious one way or the other. Minutes later my baby girl was born. She was beautiful! I cried like a baby as I continued thanking God for everything that he had done for me at that exact moment. Without him, my baby girl and I would have never made it!

Baby Miracle Jasmine Bentley ended up being 18 inches long and weighing 7 pounds and 3oz. She was healthy as can be, with beautiful big brown eyes. We named her Miracle because she definitely was that and a gift that we were told we wouldn't have. The doctors and nurses were speechless! He had no idea how the baby and I both survived. He even told himself that it had to be God. David and I just smiled and thanked the doctor for all his hard work while we continued to kiss and embrace all over our baby girl. David and I knew that it was all God and that our fate was in his hands. Our baby girl was truly a blessing. My mother, Momma Gloria, and Ms. Harrington ran into the room. They were so excited! They were not only proud of how well I did, but so filled with joy to see how precious she was. My family was complete!

23

THE AFTER

’m not going to call this the end because it’s not! This is "the after" because we are nowhere near the end of our lives and moments together. God has been too good to me for me not to tell him "thank you." God has blessed David and me with each other and a beautiful baby girl, which is definitely a bonus. We continue to grow as a family, and simply want what's best for baby Miracle Jasmine Bentley. A year after Miracle was born, my mother and stepfather, along with my baby brother, moved to the city and opened up a restaurant that I help run from time to time. My mother and I's relationship keeps getting better day by day. She is a great grandmother, and my little brother just loves the fact that he's an uncle. They both fill my heart with so much joy.

I never imagined my life would have changed dramatically, but it has and in a good way. With God all things are **Possible**! Can you believe Miracle will be five and starting school? We're all super excited for her. She's such a beautiful little girl inside and out. I'm so proud to be her mother. She reminds me so much of my Jazzy. It's like I birthed a piece of her. I still think about her to this day; I don't think

I will ever forget about her. David and I have been together now for six years, and as time goes on I learn more and more about him and vice versa. He has truly showed me how to love and trust. Love is not supposed to hurt, and I'm happy to say I no longer hurt in my heart. All tears that I shed now are always happy tears. Momma Gloria has also been a great support system, and like a second grandmother to baby Miracle, they just love each other to death. I still go down to Virginia from time to time to visit Momma Gloria; she'll always have a special place in my heart. When visiting in Virginia, I take Miracle down to the cemetery with me to see Jazzy. Even though Miracle never saw or met Jazzy before, she still feels some kind of connection to her; she calls her Aunt Jazzy, and knows that she left and went to a better place. Ms. Harrington is Miracle's godmother, and she takes Miracle every summer for a week and sees her almost every holiday.

Ms. Harrington is Miracle's godmother and takes her once a week for a sleepover for quality time. I love Ms. Harrington—or should I call her Mrs. Bentley? —to death. She truly is heaven sent. Ms. Harrington ended up marrying David's father, and is now a pastor herself and preaches the gospel right beside her husband. They are truly a man and woman of God. Not only that but true role models. Ms. Harrington still works at Sunnyside Rehabilitation Center helping young girls like myself kick off their burdens and addictions. She loves what she does and thanks God that she is as humble and obedient to his word. She is truly a willing vessel. David and I dream of having Pastor Bentley and Ms. Harrington's kind of strength; God has truly made them one. I sit back and look over my life and all the things that have happened to me and realize that I've been blessed from day one. I am who I am today because of my past;

and I'm grateful! I am no longer ashamed of who I am but grateful for who God is, because without him I would not have been able to be made whole and living the life that I am now. Lord, I thank you! Trials and tribulations may come your way, but you can and will make it as long as you have God almighty himself by your side. I'm a firm believer and witness to that! Thank you all for looking into my past life with me and seeing the glory of God master every hurt and burden in my life. To God Be the Glory!!!